That One Time I Turned into a Wolf

Leighton L. Qua

Ukiyoto Publishing

All global publishing rights are held by

Ukiyoto Publishing

Published in 2024

Content Copyright © Leighton L. Qua

ISBN 9789361722622

All rights reserved.

No part of this publication may be reproduced, transmitted, or stored in a retrieval system, in any form by any means, electronic, mechanical, photocopying, recording or otherwise, without the prior permission of the publisher.

The moral rights of the author have been asserted.

This is a work of fiction. Names, characters, businesses, places, events, locales, and incidents are either the products of the author's imagination or used in a fictitious manner. Any resemblance to actual persons, living or dead, or actual events is purely coincidental.

This book is sold subject to the condition that it shall not by way of trade or otherwise, be lent, resold, hired out or otherwise circulated, without the publisher's prior consent, in any form of binding or cover other than that in which it is published.

www.ukiyoto.com

Contents

The Strange Surprise	1
Just a Usual Morning	7
The Flood	11
The Escape from Our Cave	13
Caught!	15
The Final Great Escape	17
About the Author	20

The Strange Surprise

I woke up one morning with the wind from the window on my face. Strangely, I didn't feel cold at all; in fact, I felt warm. I removed my blanket which was harder than before. I stood up and waddled slowly to my bedroom mirror which was adjacent to my bed. Just then, I noticed that the time in my alarm clock was 3 p.m.! I then continued to walk to the mirror to fix myself up. But when I arrived at the mirror, I saw something so surprising that I gave a blank reaction. I saw a wolf!

I couldn't help my shock after a few seconds of realizing it. I jumped out of the window and ran straight towards the forest. At the first sight of it, it didn't seem as scary as it was when I was a human. I strolled around the damp forest and spotted a cave. Then an idea struck me. "Maybe this could be my new home!" I thought to myself. I sprinted into it before anyone could see me then I quickly settled in.

A few moments later, I heard approaching footsteps. They sounded scary and I didn't know what to do. I scampered to one corner of the cave as the footsteps drew closer to me. I saw a dark figure looming over me. The creature stepped out and I realized what it was…

A rhinoceros stepped out of the shadows. It quickly spotted me and ran straight for me! I stumbled away as I felt strength building up inside me. I then stopped. I looked back at the gigantic creature and immediately knew what to do.

I stood on all fours and waited for the giant figure to charge for me. Still, I stood as still as a rock and waited, and waited, and waited for the right time to come.

Finally, I knew what to do. I ran towards the rhinoceros at full sprint and took a sharp turn at the creature's butt and bit hard. By then, my mouth was full of meat. Surprisingly, it tasted good.

I stared back as the gigantic creature roared in agony before it collapsed onto the ground. I was surprised with my strength. Some thoughts came to me, "Like, I actually took down a rhinoceros all by myself?" I was shocked.

Well, since I was hungry because I skipped my morning breakfast, I inhaled my reward and swallowed it down. I then grew thirsty, so I decided to travel to the nearest clearing that I would find. A few moments later, I found a clearing. It was in the middle of the forest and the bright sunlight was reflected from the clearing to my face. Then, I took a nice refreshing drink before heading toward my cave. Although it was a long walk, I made it just before it grew dark.

I pranced into my cave and found that I was feeling rather uncomfortable. I started to scrape the ground with my claws to make a more comfortable place for me to sleep. When I was done, I felt satisfied with my work. I lay down on my side before drifting off to sleep.

The next day, I woke up. I wasn't the least bit drowsy. I was ready to start the second day of my wolf life! I felt hungry, so I went outside to hunt for breakfast.

It took a long time to find the right animal and I was honestly getting impatient. But before long, I found something meaty. Something that smelled good. It was an elephant! I charged at its bottom without even thinking. The elephant was actually harder to hunt because of its massive size, but I managed to take it down.

After taking it down, I ate all of its remains (except for the bones). I walked home swiftly after that. I had already decided to renovate my cave for a bit. After all, I still had the entire day. When I arrived, I decided to start my renovation.

First, I improved my bed. I dug my bed a little deeper and dug a few stairs to come with it. Then, when I was done, I gathered a few banana leaves and scattered them playfully on my "bed". I lay down on my bed with satisfaction. After that, I sprinted outside and dug a huge, gigantic, enormous hole in the front. I was basically trying to make my own water source! It took a long time because I had to wait for the rain.

Then, I decided to set up my own farm (since I had the skills of a human). I collected some of the seeds that I found lying around in random places. I dug up tiny holes and buried the seeds there. I was done! Finally!

I then noticed an unusual ruffle in the grass. I saw a black outline of something slithering towards me. I immediately knew it was a snake. I slipped into my cave where there was no grass at all. After a few seconds, the biggest snake I had ever seen in my entire life sprang up on me! It had a long scaly body and a terrifying look.

I quickly dodged the attack. I then had this feeling inside me that was urging me to go forward and defeat the snake! After all, this couldn't be the end of my life. I was new to being a wolf. I like being a wolf; I didn't want to change anything about it. I lunged forward as the snake opened its mouth to reveal its sharp threatening fangs!

I got frightened because the snake was stronger than I thought. But still, I didn't give up. I dashed for the snake and leaped with all my strength. In the air, I raised my mighty head and prepared to bite the terrifying snake.

I then made a landing and swiped the helpless snake with the last drop of my energy. I felt so tired after that, so I carelessly dropped the snake on the ground who managed to scratch me with one of its fangs.

That woke me up. And I was quick. I pierced my claws through the snake who gave an unbearable shriek. I surrendered as the snake stared daggers at me before dying.

Well, I actually survived! That was a close one! I slept well that night, excited about what adventures I might encounter tomorrow.

6 That One Time I Turned into a Wolf

Just a Usual Morning

I awoke in the forest, as usual. I stretched out and realized that it was raining hard last night. I was filled with delight as I remembered that I had set up a farm and my own water source the other day. I walked to the front of my cave and looked right, finding that my water source was filled to the brim with fresh glittering water. Then, I looked to my left and saw fresh green plants.

Just then, my nose caught a light smell floating through the winds. I followed it to find a tasty looking moose going on with its business. I sneaked up behind him, waiting for the right time.

When the right time came, I took a run for it and ran up the steep body of the moose. When I arrived at the top, I pounced on his butt and ate from there.

Then I traveled back to my cave to take a long, refreshing drink from my own pond. I decided to take a stroll around the forest after that. I slowly walked at first, but then I started to run around using up all my energy.

Just then, I heard a familiar howl. It sounded like the howls that I made. I then noticed a ruffling in the nearby bushes. I wasn't sure about my decision, but I leapt forward and pounced on the bush. Just then, a wolf came leaping out of the bushes, wide-eyed.

"W-w-who are you?" the other wolf asked.

"Well," I said, "I'm a wolf and…" At that moment I realized that the wolf could talk! "Wait, you can talk?" I asked, shocked.

"Yes, I can. Did you just suddenly turn into a wolf too?" asked the other wolf.

"Yes," I said.

And that was where our conversation started. The other wolf introduced herself saying that her name was Patricia. Patricia explained to me that she was homeless and didn't have a place to stay. I invited her to live with me and she agreed.

I took her to my cave, and I said, "This is my house, Patricia. You can stay wherever you want."

Patricia chose to stay at the far end of the cave, just beside me. I helped her build a bed and even collected some banana leaves for her bed.

Patricia then said, "Arachnee (my name), I'm getting hungry. Want to go hunt out?"

"All right, sure," I replied.

Patricia and I began to stroll around the forest looking for some food. Just then, Patricia and I found a tiger. I surrendered as Patricia motioned for me to follow her. I found out that she was fond of hunting big and powerful creatures that were aggressive. So, what could I do?

Patricia and I leaped forward at the same time. She took the front side while I took the back side. I tackled the tiger with my talents, at the same time watching her wrestle with the mighty tiger.

I managed to flip the tiger's back legs over. The tiger growled angrily as he turned to face me.

"JUST AIM FOR THE NECK!" Patricia hollered at me.

I did what she said and wounded the tiger with one of my sharp claws. The tiger stopped trying to attack me for a bit, so Patricia and I pounced on the weak tiger. Patricia then bit the tiger's butt as I held the tiger still through his neck. The tiger collapsed onto the ground as Patricia and I collided and fell down.

After that, we went home together. We entered our cave and ended the day getting ourselves comfortable in our beds.

That One Time I Turned into a Wolf

The Flood

I woke up the next morning to find that our cave was flooded. What's more, it was raining. Patricia wasn't awake yet, but I swam outside to find something that could block the water from coming in. I then felt like building something.

So, I went back inside my cave and started to dig beside my bed. I dug and dug until I reached the outside of my cave. I then started to dig a huge hole. Before long, the large hole was filled with water. The water went back to where I started to dig. Beside my bed. Now, I could drink water without going out anymore!

Soon, Patricia woke up. She was frightened of the overflowing water, but I explained to her what happened.

"What's happening? Why is our cave overflowing?" Patricia asked.

"I woke up like this and I think it's been raining all night," I answered.

"What will we do then?"

"Maybe we can find something to block the entrance to our cave?"

"Okay, but I want 🍞 🍚 🍪 🍋 🍗 🍔 🍕 after."

"Okay, let's find something to block the entrance of our cave first."

Together, we found a huge rock and used it to block the entrance of our cave. We then found another rock to block the hole leading to the inside of our cave.

"OKAY, NOW LET'S EAT," said Patricia in a loud voice.

"Okay," I said.

But then I realized that it was flooding outside, and the entrance was blocked by a huge rock. Patricia flashed me an angry look, as she figured out what I was thinking.

.

The Escape from Our Cave

Patricia and I began to try to push the rock to make it budge a tiny bit. But despite our efforts, it did not move. Then, I remembered the hole I dug a few moments ago before Patricia woke up. I showed the hole to her and told her, "Maybe we can get out of here through this hole."

"Oh, ok," Patricia replied.

I held my breath as I plunged into the water. I felt a cool gush along my heels as I lunged into the water. Then, with the help of my four legs, I swam around the passage. At first, I was a little lost. Eventually, I pushed myself upward toward the other end of the tunnel and climbed out.

Then, I realized that the flooding had gotten a lot higher than a while ago. So, I had to swim around for a while until I got used to it. Suddenly, I remembered Patricia who was still inside the cave. I called to her in the loudest voice I could for her to come to me.

A few seconds later, a head emerged from the tunnel. I immediately knew it was Patricia. She then swam up to me.

"How will we catch our food now?" she asked.

"We can probably find some fish," I suggested.

"Where do we find fishes?"

"Probably near the lake where they live."

"All right."

Patricia and I swam toward the lake and found schools of fish swimming around in confusion. Patricia and I caught a few unfortunate fishes before heading back towards our cave.

Caught!

As Patricia and I walked back to our cave, I noticed the leaves ruffling unusually. I took one step forward, but suddenly, the world started turning! Patricia and I were squeezed together tightly in a tight space, and we were very confused. We started whirling around in large circles; I closed my eyes uncomfortably. Suddenly, the world stopped turning, and Patricia and I stopped whirling in big circles.

I opened one eye, even though I was still very dizzy, and glanced at Patricia. Seeing that she was dazed, I looked away and realized that we were hanging from a tree! Suddenly, I felt myself moving downwards and getting closer to the ground. Then, I realized that Patricia and I were hanging in a net and that this was a trap!

Patricia opened her eyes slowly, and as I did too, I could see her confusion. We looked around, realizing that we were in a strange vehicle getting carried to an unknown place.

After a few moments, we were pulled out of the vehicle and were dragged into a blue tent with red stripes on it. That's when I realized that we were in a circus!

"Patricia, are you awake?" I asked.

"Umm, yes," replied Patricia, clearly very dizzy, "Are we at the circus?"

"Yes," I replied, "I think they are gonna try to train us to join a show!"

"That's cool, but I heard the animals here aren't treated very well."

"Oh no, we need to find a way to escape!"

That was all we were able to say to each other before we were thrown into different cage cells. I couldn't bear to open my eyes when this happened, so I closed them the entire time. But when I finally opened my eyes, I realized that Patricia was nowhere to be found.

I should have kept my eyes open, I thought to myself. I frantically searched for a way to escape and find Patricia. Suddenly, I found a lock outside the cage. I desperately yanked it with my teeth and grinded it. Finally, I freed myself. I ran around as fast as my legs could carry me.

The Final Great Escape

I ran around the circus trying to find Patricia, but I couldn't. I figured that the humans would start looking for me soon, so I decided to look around as fast as possible. Just then, I remembered something.

I reared my head back and howled as loud as I could. I heard Patricia howl back. I followed the sound and found her. She was chained to the ground. I quickly unchained her, and we ran out of the circus unnoticed. We ran back to the forest together, until Patricia found something that wasn't there before. There was an old cottage with a witch standing outside.

Patricia and I came closer to the witch, at the same time, making sure that the witch couldn't see us. We immediately heard the witch talking to her pet cat, which was sitting on a nearby windowsill.

"I wonder what happened to those two little girls," she said with an evil grin on her face.

"Oh, the ones you turned into wolves?" asked the cat.

"I actually still have the antidote," the witch replied, "It's at the top of my brewery table beside my gazing ball."

The two laughed hard as Patricia and I sneaked into the witch's cottage. Once we got in, we immediately found the magic potion on a nearby table. The problem was it was way too high for both of us to reach. We started to think of way, but then the door opened, and the witch came inside!

Luckily, we were quick and scampered behind an old bookshelf. The witch, having very bad eyesight, did not notice anything. She just walked by the bookshelf and went to the other room which was labeled: "Experiment Room". When Patricia and I came out from our hiding place, we discovered that the witch had taken the potion with her!

Without even thinking, we rushed into the experiment room and grabbed the potion from the witch's hand. The witch screamed as Patricia and I ran as fast as our legs could carry us. Although we were running really fast, the witch was catching up. She immediately summoned her magic broom to help her go faster.

Eventually, the witch caught up. But then, Patricia accidentally dropped the potion which she was holding in her mouth. There was a puff of smoke. There was a lot of coughing and confusion.

Finally, after what seemed to take years, the smoke cleared, and everyone could see each other again. Except, that . . . Patricia and I felt very different.

As we stood up, we realized that we were humans again. Then, we looked at the witch who had now become a wolf.

About the Author

Leighton Qua

Leighton Qua is a Grade 5 student who lives in the Philippines. She enjoys writing, telling stories, and traveling to different places around the world. She is a fan of dragons and anything purple. She often reads books written by Rick Riordan and Pseudonymous Bosch. Currently, she has already written two storybooks, *That One Time I Turned into a Wolf* and *Adventures of Esperanza*.

www.ingramcontent.com/pod-product-compliance
Lightning Source LLC
LaVergne TN
LVHW041603070526
838199LV00047B/2116